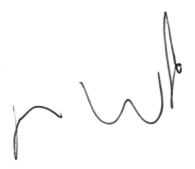

And Then It Happened
..2..

AND THEN IT HAPPENED

HAPPENED

·· 2 ··

M & L Wade

Books for Boys

ISBN 0-9731178-1-8

Printed in Canada

Books for Boys
P.O. Box 87
Strathroy ON N7G 3J1

Two Are Editurs

Contents

Chapter 1

Sleigh-Riding

It was December 26th. Christmas was over and we were on Christmas break for two whole glorious weeks. By now, most of the skin had grown back on Gordon's cheek, and we were pulling our toboggans up the hill behind the barn on Paulo's farm. We had been tobogganing here for years, and every year we got more and more daring. This year we had built snow ramps, and as we sailed down the hill we would hit a ramp, become airborne, and then come crashing down, causing hats and gloves and boots to fly in all directions. Another great tobogganing game was to whiz down the hill from three different directions at the same time, crashing our sleighs and bodies together in a three toboggan pile-up.

We had spent the entire cold, windy day playing tobogganing games. After hours of sledding, the hill was a smooth, fast, icy sheet of glass, and by dusk, we were ready for our final assault down the hill. With the three of us on one toboggan, we aimed toward the largest ramp to see how high we could launch ourselves and still manage to land in one piece. We seated ourselves aerodynamically on the toboggan, with Paulo in the lead and Gordon in the rear. We eased the tip of the toboggan over the top of the hill. On the count of three, Gordon pushed us off. The frigid air stung the raw skin of our cheeks and noses as we raced down the hill toward the ramp, and suddenly we saw it. A herd of cows had emerged from the woods and was trudging its way slowly toward the barn for the evening. The entire herd was directly in our path! A second later, our toboggan hit the ramp and we were airborne. We hovered for an agonizing moment in the air and then landed with a bone-jarring *thud* right in the middle of the startled herd. The terrified cattle reacted as if a giant pterodactyl had swooped out of the sky and suddenly landed in their midst, and it was every cow for itself as the animals scrambled to safety. Clinging to the sleigh for dear life, we found ourselves in the middle of a stampede. Dodging cow patties and hooves, our sleigh glided through the herd, overtaking several mooing and bawling cows. And then it happened. The sleigh's tow rope came loose and got tangled around the hind leg of a huge bull as he raced full-speed toward the barn. The poor bull doubled his efforts to get away, dragging the toboggan and the three of us behind him at a terrifying speed. Racing past the barn, the frightened animal changed direction suddenly and headed straight toward Paulo's house. Seeing the fence, he changed direction again, causing the tow rope to snap and launching us through the air, over the fence, and straight toward the Lima's living room window. Covering my face with my wet mittens, I heard a terrible crashing sound as we smashed through the glass and flew right into the huge Christmas tree that stood in the centre of the room. The tree toppled over, crushing ornaments and presents, and Gordon, Paulo and I were thrown in a heap onto the living room sofa. I was dazed. Paulo was stunned. Gordon yelled, "Cool! Let's do that again!"

And then we heard yelling of another kind. Running into the room, Paulo's mother let out a shriek as she saw our trail of destruction. I cringed and tried to sink deeper into the sofa for safety. Paulo froze, terrified at the thought of what his mother would do next. It was Gordon, who had talked his way out of many such scrapes, who saved the day. He looked straight at Mrs. Lima and explained at length how the bull had pulled us across the yard, and that we were lucky to still be alive after our death-defying ordeal. When he finished, even Paulo and I had a tear in our eye. Best of all, Mrs. Lima was no longer angry, but relieved and thankful that we had escaped without even so much as a cut.

Chapter 2

Snow Day

Last night after supper, it started to snow, and by bedtime, a blizzard was raging outside. During the night the snow continued to pile up.

I awoke the next morning to the sound of a radio and the smell of bacon wafting from the kitchen. *Bacon on a Thursday? That's odd*, I thought. No one in our house had time to cook bacon on a school day. Then I remembered the storm! I jumped out of bed and ran down the hall. In the kitchen, my mother greeted me with the nicest words a kid could hear. No, it wasn't *"I love you"*, or even *"We're going to raise your allowance."* It was *"School's been cancelled. It's a snow day!"*

The phone rang as I was enjoying my bacon and toast. It was Gordon.

"Isn't it great?" he shouted. "What do you wanna do first?"

Half an hour later, he arrived at my back door, his sled in tow. It was another thirty minutes before Paulo arrived.

"Wow, is it ever deep!" he said, out of breath from his long walk. "And it's still coming down. Maybe school will be cancelled tomorrow, too!" That's what I like about Paulo; He always thinks positively!

We trudged down my street, waving to Mr. Butterworth who was out snow-blowing his driveway, and then we headed towards Danglemore Public School. The yard was filled with kids sliding and tobogganing down the hill at the back of the schoolyard, an area which was normally out of bounds.

"It's too crowded," said Gordon. "Let's go see if the

river's frozen."

We set off through the snow again, and we soon came to the river. It was partially frozen over, and ice grew out from the shore.

"Do you think it's thick enough to walk out on?" asked Paulo.

"I don't know," I replied. I carefully put my foot on the ice and tested it, ready to jump back if I heard it crack. The ice held. Holding Paulo's outstretched had, I took a few more steps.

"It's OK!" I called, venturing out further. Gordon and Paulo joined me. With the wind and snow whipping around us, we walked and slid on the ice until we came to a bend in the river. And then it happened. A loud snapping sound caused us all to turn and look back in the direction we had just come from. With sudden horror, we realized that we were moving!

"Holy cow!" Paulo shouted. "The ice broke off from shore and we're floating down-river!"

The shore was now three metres away and it was too far to jump across the deep, freezing cold water. We stood on the ice, helplessly floating away from town. We were doomed. We scanned the shore, hoping to see someone, *anyone*, who could help us, but the storm was keeping everyone safely indoors. We sat down dejectedly on the ice and watched the shore slip by.

After several long minutes of silence, I said that we'd probably only drift for a few minutes before someone noticed us and came to our rescue. Paulo said he thought we'd be stuck all day 'til our families noticed us missing. They'd call 911 and our pictures would be on the six o'clock news. Gordon said he thought we'd probably freeze to death long before anyone found us. We'd drift out to the open sea where sailors would discover our stiff, frozen bodies huddled together as we tried in vain to keep warm before finally succumbing to a slow, painful death on a patch of ice. *Not a cheering thought.*

We drifted down river for what felt like hours when suddenly we noticed that the river had narrowed and we were now very close to shore. Less than two metres of water separated us from dry land.

"It's our only chance," said Paulo, and on the count of

three, we jumped for it, landing half in and half out of the frigid water. We quickly scampered up the snow-covered bank.

We were alive and safe, but we were freezing, wet and lost, and the snow continued to fall. Ahead of us was a field, and at the far end of it, we could just make out a farmhouse.

"L-L-Let's see if anyone's home," I stammered through chattering teeth.

Twenty minutes later, we were standing on the front porch and Gordon rang the bell with his frozen mitt.

It took only seconds for the door to swing open, and there, to our great surprise and horror, stood our teacher, Mrs. Hoagsbrith!

Looking equally surprised and horrified, she gasped, "What are you boys doing here? And why are your jeans frozen solid?"

In a rush of words, we told our story as she ushered us into the warm house. When we finished, she shook her head and told us to get out of our wet clothes. Gordon, Paulo and I glanced nervously at each other. What would we put on? We had no spare clothes! But Mrs. Hoagsbrith was already busy pulling off our wet hats and frozen mitts, and then she led us into the laundry room at the back of the house.

"Now, get undressed and put all your wet clothing in the dryer, and wrap yourselves up in these towels," she said, pointing to a pile of neatly-folded towels. "And then come into the kitchen for some hot chocolate."

Ten minutes later, clutching our towels tightly around us, we sat down on Mrs. Hoagsbrith's kitchen chairs. Mrs. Hoagsbrith left to turn on the dryer, and when she returned, we called our parents. Our teacher spoke to each of them in turn, telling them that we were safe from harm but would have to spend the night at her farmhouse and probably part of the next day, too, because her road certainly wouldn't be plowed for several days.

"Cheer up, boys," said Mrs. Hoagsbrith when she hung up the phone and saw the looks on our faces. "When your clothes are dry, you can shovel my driveway, and then when you're finished that, I'd be happy to teach you the English and Math lessons I had planned for today."

10

Mrs. Hoagsbrith grinned her best teacher smile, and she gave a contented sigh.

Chapter 3

Bear Day

It was April 1st, and I had just celebrated my birthday. I got the usual stuff - money, clothes, some CDs, and a neat book on animal tracks and how to identify them. Gordon, Paulo and I were in my bedroom, eating the last of the pizza and birthday cake. Gordon seemed particularly interested in my new book, and, quite out of character, he was awfully quiet.

Finally, he closed the book and said with a look in his eye I knew all too well, "Boys, am I brilliant, or what?

Listen to this!" Gordon was famous for coming up with truly unique and wonderful ideas, so I turned down the music blaring from my CD player, and Paulo and I turned eager eyes towards him.

"I've been looking at these bear tracks, and they don't look as if they'd be too hard to make."

"Why would anyone want to make bear tracks?" Paulo asked.

"Well," explained Gordon slowly. "If we had our own set of bear tracks, we could make tracks all over town. People would think a bear was prowling around. People might not feel safe, and they wouldn't want to send their kids to school. They'd be scared that the bear might attack their kids on their way to school or standing around waiting for the bus. *They might even have to close the school until the bear was caught.*"

"Close the school because of fake bear tracks? What a great idea!" I exclaimed.

We set to work immediately. Rolling out some plasticine, we carefully made the impression of a bear's paw - a *big* bear's paw. Next, we poured in lots of modelling plastic, which would have to dry overnight. We hid our bear paw in the back of my closet, away from the prying eyes of my sister and parents, and Gordon and Paulo headed home.

Early the next morning, I quietly climbed out of bed and opened the closet. I pulled out the bear paw and was pleased to see that the modelling plastic was dry. I gently peeled away the plasticine. In my hands I held a huge bear paw with five long, deadly claws. *It was perfect!* I phoned Paulo and Gordon, and we arranged to meet that afternoon to plot our strategy.

There were lots of muddy places around town since it was spring and it had been raining for weeks. With our bear paw well-concealed in a plastic bag, we hopped on our bikes and headed towards the outskirts of town. At the farm beside Paulo's, we stopped and leaned our bikes against a tree. Checking to see that no one was watching, we crawled under the fence and darted across the field. I pulled the bear paw out of the bag and carefully made one giant track in the mud near the barn. With hearts pounding, we raced back to our bikes and pedalled away, not daring to look back. Next, we headed to town and toward the park, where we made some more tracks in the gardens. At the side of the road, we stopped and made several tracks in the soft shoulder. We also wanted to make sure that kids would spot the tracks on their way to school the next day, so we made a few near the school, as well. Then, grinning from ear to ear, we headed for home. I carefully hid the bear paw in my closet and waited for Monday.

The next morning, Gordon, Paulo and I were the first kids at school. We didn't want to miss one bit of the excitement. Within a few minutes, several more kids arrived. They obviously hadn't noticed our tracks, because no one said anything. Then suddenly, we heard a lady screech near the entrance of the school. We looked over to see a mom clutching her four-year-old.

"Quick! Somebody call the principal! Call the police!" she shrilled. People came from all directions to see what the commotion was about. Teachers and parents came out of nowhere, and soon the principal was on the scene. Somebody must have called 911 because two

15

police cars and a fire-truck roared down the road a few minutes later, sirens wailing. *This was great! Even better than we had anticipated!!* One police officer yelled something to another officer who ran over to his car and returned with a bullhorn. He ordered all of us to go into the school immediately. Gordon, Paulo and I raced to our classroom and watched the action from the window. More police cars filled the streets, picking up kids and delivering them to school. At nine o'clock, the principal announced that a bear had wandered into town, and that the police were searching for it. We would have indoor recesses until further notice.

"I thought you said we'd get a day *off* school, not be trapped *in* school!" I hissed at Gordon. Gordon merely shrugged.

At the end of the day, the principal made another announcement. He said that the bear had not been caught yet, but that the police think he wandered out of town again, based on some new tracks spotted by a farmer. It would be safe to walk home, but we were to stay inside once we got there, just in case.

The three of us quickly biked to my house. We pulled the bear paw out of the closet and stared at it with admiration. Our next plan was to have Gordon make tracks in his own neighbourhood so it would appear that the bear had come back into town. An hour later, Gordon pedalled home for dinner with the bear paw hidden in his knap-sack.

Later that night as I was doing my homework, I heard something on the T.V. news that made me stop and listen. The announcer was talking about bear tracks that had been found just outside of town by a farmer. The farm flashed on the screen, and suddenly there it was - our very own bear track! Next, the announcer said that tracks had recently been discovered in a neighbourhood near Danglemore Public School. The scene on the T.V. changed, and there was Gordon's street, followed by more close-ups of the bear track.

"A woman claims that at approximately five o'clock this afternoon, she returned from the grocery store to find two large bear tracks under her kitchen window," the newscaster said. "Police are investigating, and it appears as though the bear is back. Residents are warned to stay indoors and to notify police if they sight the bear." Then, unbelievably, came an eye-witness account from a man who claimed he actually *saw* the bear.

People's imaginations are really running away with them, I thought. *This is too good! Now they'll really have to cancel school!*

Sure enough, when I came into the kitchen the next morning, my sister greeted me with the news that school was indeed cancelled.

"Great!" I said, trying to look surprised. Turning to my mother, I asked, "Can Gordon and Paulo spend the day over here if their parents'll drive them?"

My mother gave this careful consideration, and finally she said "I guess it will be OK, if your sister doesn't mind keeping an eye on you."

"What?!" I shrieked. "We're not babies! We don't need a babysitter."

"And I wanted to go to Jessica's," added my sister.

My mother started to protest, but was shouted down by my sister and me. Finally she gave in. "Alright, but I'm

18

going to call you at noon to make sure everything's OK and that you're still in the house." She gave me a warning look. I smiled innocently. After all, what trouble could the three of us get into?

Fifteen minutes later Gordon and Paulo were dropped off at my house, and my sister left with my mother.

We spent the morning lounging around the house watching T.V., eating and playing games. It was the good life! After lunch, Gordon suggested that we make some fresh tracks to keep the police searching and to make sure school was closed for another day.

"How?" demanded Paulo. "We can't leave the house."

"Hmmm," said Gordon, as he stared out the window. "I have a plan. We could go out the back door and sneak into Mr. Butterworth's backyard. No one would see us from the road. We'll make some tracks in the dirt near his garbage can. Then we'll tie some fishing line to the handle on the can and run back into your yard. Then we'll yank the fishing line and knock over the garbage can. Old Mr. Butterworth will come running outside to see what the noise is all about and he'll spot the bear

19

tracks! He'll call the police for sure."

It was a good plan. A few minutes later, we were crouched in the bushes that ran beside the two houses, and I gave the fishing line a good tug. The garbage can fell over with a loud crash, spewing garbage all over Mr. Butterworth's patio. In a flash, the back door of his house flew open, and out came Mr. Butterworth, expecting to see a stray dog running away, or maybe one of us kids. But then he spied the bear tracks, and he quickly backed into his house, his eyes darting all over his yard. We could hardly contain our laughter as we crawled across the lawn and back into my house. A few minutes later we heard the wail of a siren, and then we saw a police van pull into the driveway next door. An officer stepped out of the van and walked around to the back of the vehicle. He opened the door and the next moment we drew in our breath as the police officer led two large dogs on leashes around to the back of Mr. Butterworth's house.

In a trembling voice, Paulo said, "The police have tracking dogs. They'll lead them right to your back door!"

We watched as the dogs sniffed around the garbage can, and then headed toward the bushes where we had hidden. A moment later, they were in our backyard, and then it happened. We all jumped as we heard a heavy knock at the back door.

"Open up. This is the police. " We froze, not even daring to breathe.

"Oh, they're home, all right," said a voice. It was Mr. Butterworth! "The young one and his buddies. I saw them get dropped off here earlier."

The pounding came again.

"We gotta let the police in," said Paulo, panic in his voice.

Slowly, I walked to the door and opened it a crack. "Who's there?" I asked, trembling.

"The police, and I need to talk to you kids."

I opened the door to let the officer in, and what I saw caused my blood to run cold.

"Does this belong to one of you?" the officer demanded, and he held up our bear paw.

"I thought you brought it in with you," whispered

Gordon.

"I thought you had it!" Paulo shot back. In our haste, we had left the bear paw lying right in the bushes! We were doomed. Just then, the phone rang. It was mom! We were *really* doomed!

The police insisted on talking to my mother, who said she'd be right home. In fact, all of our parents were called. I would have given anything to be back in school at that moment.

"First dead birds, and now a fake bear!" scolded the officer, shaking his head. "Do you kids realize how much work you've caused the police force? Do you think we have nothing better to do than run around town chasing fake bear tracks?" Boy, were we in a mess. We were sent to my room while our parents talked to the police for almost half an hour - the longest half hour of my life.

Finally we were ordered back into the living room and stood on trembling legs before the police and our parents. Our sentence was worse than anything we had imagined. The police officer told us that we had to go on the six o'clock news and apologize to the entire town for what we had done, and the rest would be up to our parents. I opened my mouth to protest, but then I caught the look in my mother's eye.

"What time do you want us at the T.V. station, officer?" I asked meekly.

Chapter 4

The Naked Parrot

Despite being a grown-up, Gordon's Uncle Ivan is one of the neatest guys I know. In fact, he's so cool, he doesn't even seem like a real grown-up. But he has a truck and a house and he's going slightly bald, all of which definitely make him a grown-up. He doesn't even mind us kids hanging around him when he comes to visit Gordon's family. In fact, he would rather be outside playing soccer with us or pulling practical jokes than sitting through long, boring dinners listening to long, boring adult conversations. He isn't at all interested in

24

Aunt Millie's hernia operation or Uncle What's-his-name's hip replacement. That's why when Gordon told us that his uncle was bringing his new girlfriend to dinner on Sunday to meet the family, we were shocked. This sounded serious and we knew it meant trouble. This called for action. What we needed was a plan.

"Maybe you could tell your uncle there's no room at the table for another person," Paulo suggested.

"My mom's dying to meet her," said Gordon glumly. "She thinks it's time her brother settled down and got married."

We were sitting in Gordon's room trying to come up with a good plan, when suddenly a loud squawk filled the air, making us all jump. It was Gordon's pet parrot, Archie. Archie once had a disease that caused him to lose all his feathers. He was fine now, but his feathers never grew back. He was quite a sight, and could actually give you quite a scare if you weren't warned ahead of time. Archie didn't talk much, either. Most parrots repeat what they hear, but the only thing Archie ever said was "Help me!". Then again, you'd say "help me," too, if you had to live in Gordon's room. The really neat thing about Archie, though, was that he could do some cool tricks. For example, he could play dead when commanded to do so. Gordon would say, "Archie, play dead" and the parrot would flop over on his back and lie there for a few seconds, his feet sticking straight up in the air. Archie let out another squawk, and a look came into Gordon's eye that I knew only too well.

"Am I brilliant, or what?" asked Gordon when he finished explaining his plan to us. I had to hand it to Gordon; The plan was beautiful.

Sunday finally arrived. Gordon had asked his mom if Paulo and I could have dinner with the family, to help make Uncle Ivan's girlfriend feel really welcome.

"That would be lovely, dear," she crooned. "Just as long as you three stay out of trouble and don't pester your uncle."

"We could even help you serve dinner, and afterwards, we'll help you clear the table and do the dishes," offered Paulo. *Dishes! No one said anything about dishes,* I thought. I wasn't so sure I liked this plan after all.

26

"That would be nice," said Gordon's mom quickly.

"What's for dinner, anyway?" asked Gordon

"Roast chicken, mashed potatoes, gravy, vegetables, salad, and for dessert, apple pie."

Mmmm. It sounded delicious.

At quarter to six on Sunday, Gordon, Paulo and I crouched by the living room window, waiting for Uncle Ivan. At five minutes to six, a shiny blue truck slowed down in front of the house and pulled into the driveway. We stared at the unfamiliar vehicle.

"Must be someone turning around," said Gordon.

"No! It's your uncle!" exclaimed Paulo.

"Is that what colour his truck is?" I asked. Gordon's uncle had the neatest truck. You could eat candy or chips or pop in the truck and just toss the wrappers over your shoulder into the back. He didn't mind at all.

"I always thought his truck was gray," said Paulo.

"It's been washed! I bet *she* made him do it!" spat Gordon.

We continued to peer out of the window, trying to get a glimpse of the new girlfriend. We figured she'd be old and mean. When she stepped out of the truck, however, she looked quite young, and she was laughing at something Uncle Ivan had just said. The two of them held hands as they came up the front walk.

At the sound of the doorbell, Gordon's mom sailed into the hallway and threw open the front door.

"You must be Jennifer," she sang. "Come right in. We're so pleased that Ivan brought you. Here, let me take your coat. Is it cold outside? My, what a pretty sweater. I hope you like roast chicken. It's Ivan's favourite."

When she finally ran out of breath, Uncle Ivan said, "Hello, Claire. Dinner smells great! By the way, how's Uncle Mel's new hip?"

It was worse than we thought! Time for action.

When Uncle Ivan, Jennifer and the rest of the family were seated in the dining room, Paulo and I offered to help carry bowls and platters from the kitchen to the dining room.

"Thanks for your help, boys . I'll carry this last platter into the dining room. It's very heavy," said Gordon's mom.

Thinking quickly, I said, " Don't you want to take off your apron first, Mrs. Smith?"

She looked down at herself and laughed. "You're right! I forgot I still had it on." She handed me the platter piled high with roast chicken, and I quickly darted out of the kitchen with it. Instead of going into the dining room, however, I made a quick u-turn into the living room, and Gordon ducked into the dining room carrying Paulo's mom's covered silver platter. He placed it on the table and pulled off the lid just as his mother came into the dining room. What she saw caused her to stop dead in her tracks. There, on the middle of the platter, was Archie, lying on his back with his feet sticking straight up in the air! Jennifer gasped, as did Gordon's sisters. And then it happened. Archie jumped up and yelled "Help me! Help me!" and he began running around on top of the table.

"Get that *s!@*! naked parrot off our dinner table!" bellowed Mr. Smith. The girls shrieked, scaring Archie and causing him to run faster. Water glasses were knocked over and dinner rolls were sent flying. The three of us ran around the table trying to catch Archie. He made a quick turn and headed straight toward Jennifer, who shrieked and tried to push her chair back from the table. It toppled over, taking Jennifer with it. Uncle Ivan jumped up to help Jennifer, and poor Archie was so frightened he hopped into a bowl of mashed potatoes and got stuck. Gordon grabbed the bird and plucked him out of the potatoes. Two of Gordon's sisters were standing on their chairs, screaming, and Gordon's mother was too horrified to speak. Gordon stood there, holding Archie, dripping mashed potatoes on the rug.

What happened next was nothing short of a miracle, and is the reason why, to this day, we really like Aunt Jennifer.

Jennifer started to giggle, just quietly at first, but then Uncle Ivan joined in, and then Paulo and I burst out laughing. Soon everyone but Gordon's mom was roaring with uncontrollable laughter.

"That was the best practical joke I ever saw," exclaimed Jennifer through her laughter. "It makes me homesick for my little brother. He's always pulling stunts like this."

"I have to hand it to you three. This tops anything I've ever pulled," said Uncle Ivan.

As for Gordon, Paulo and me, we were forced to clean up the entire mess, wash all the dishes *and* apologize to Gordon's mother before we could have a single piece of cold roast chicken and apple pie.

Chapter 5

The Giant Gerbil

One Friday afternoon, our teacher, Mrs. Hoagsbrith, stood at the front of the class and held up a box containing a tiny, one-day old baby gerbil, eyes still shut.

"This will be our science project for the next month," she announced. "Starting today, we will study the growth and development of a gerbil." Two months ago, we had done a similar project with a goldfish named Lucky. I glanced over at his bowl and watched him swimming around as the teacher continued. "We will keep a daily record of his weight and length. For now, he will have to

be fed with an eye-dropper and kept warm, which means
that one of you will have to take him home for the
weekend to care for him."

Every hand in the room shot up, so Mrs. Hoagsbrith
wrote a number on a piece of paper and we each got one
guess. When it was Gordon's turn, he guessed 88, the
number of his favourite hockey player. With a loud sigh,
Mrs. Hoagsbrith handed the box to Gordon, along with a
list of instructions.

"Remember, it is important to keep him warm. This is
our science project for the next month, and nothing must
happen to the gerbil while he's in your care," warned the
teacher.

Next, the class voted on a name for the baby gerbil.
When the bell rang, Gordon slung his back-pack over his
shoulder and carefully picked up the box containing the
gerbil.

"Come on, Squeak," he said. "Wait till you meet my
pet parrot!"

Mrs. Hoagsbrith opened her mouth to say something,
but closed it again and sat down wearily at her desk.

Paulo and I walked to Gordon's house with him and carefully carried the box up to Gordon's room. Gordon gently placed it on his bed and we admired the tiny, helpless gerbil. A sudden loud squawk from Archie, Gordon's featherless parrot, made us all turn our attention to the large cage across the room.

"Help me!" screeched the bird.

"He wants to be fed," said Gordon as he pulled out a bag of birdseed and began filling a plastic bowl in Archie's cage.

While we were busy with Archie, none of us saw Gordon's dog Chopper come into the room. None of us saw him walk over to the bed and sniff Squeak, and none of us saw him reach out his long pink tongue and quickly lap up the tiny gerbil, swallowing him whole in a single gulp. We turned around just in time to see the dog licking his chops in satisfaction.

"NO!" yelled Gordon as the three of us rushed over to the bed. We peered into the empty box and then pounced on the dog.

"Spit it out!!" yelled Gordon, prying Chopper's mouth

open with his fingers. We peered into the dog's empty mouth.

"It's too late," moaned Paulo. "Squeak is a goner!"

"What am I gonna do?" cried Gordon. "The teacher's gonna kill me!!"

We were silent for a moment, and then Paulo exclaimed, "I know! Our barn is full of rats. If we can find one of their nests, we can substitute a baby rat for Squeak. No one will know the difference!"

It was a great idea! First thing the next morning, Gordon and I biked over to Paulo's house and we began hunting for baby rats. We soon found a large nest down by the sewer drain with seven baby rats and no sign of their mother. Gordon reached into the nest and plucked out a tiny rat.

"No one will ever know," he said, placing it into the gerbil's box.

Gordon spent the rest of the weekend caring for the baby barn rat, Squeak II, as we secretly called him, keeping him warm and well away from Chopper. He was relieved to deliver the tiny creature to school on Monday, and we considered the whole matter closed.

Unfortunately, we hadn't considered what would happen when the rat started to grow. The difference between a full-grown gerbil and a full-grown rat is like the difference between a horse and an elephant!

Everyday the class monitored Squeak's progress, carefully measuring and weighing him. We kept track of how much food he ate, and by the end of the first full week, our teacher seemed very pleased.

"Class, this is a very healthy gerbil. He's growing faster than I've ever seen. You're all doing a fine job!"

Over the weekend, Squeak continued to grow, and by Monday, Mrs. Hoagsbrith announced in a puzzled voice that the gerbil had already reached his full adult size and weight.

"I've never seen anything like it," she told us, frowning.

We continued to weigh and measure Squeak all week because the gerbil continued to grow. By the following Monday, Mrs. Hoagsbrith announced that our gerbil was three times bigger than a normal gerbil. His tail and whiskers were also unusually long for a gerbil. She shot a suspicious glance at Gordon.

"Gordon," she said. "This isn't the baby gerbil I gave you to take care of two weeks ago, is it?"

With a sigh, Gordon took a deep breath and explained to the class how his dog had eaten the baby gerbil, and that he had replaced it with a barn rat. He thankfully left Paulo and me out of his story.

There were loud gasps and snickers of laughter that were quickly silenced with a glance from Mrs. Hoagsbrith. The teacher took a deep breath and sighed.

"It's too bad about Squeak, but I guess our science project isn't totally ruined. We can study a barn rat instead, I guess. Accidents do happen, I suppose."

Accidents do happen? What was wrong with Mrs. Hoagsbrith? She didn't even seem mad! She must be getting soft in her old age.

Our class rat continued to grow at an amazing pace, but when he began biting at kids who came near his cage, Mrs. Hoagsbrith announced that the science project was over, and that Gordon was to return the rat to wherever it came from. And then it happened.

A gerbil cage is designed to hold a gerbil, not a huge barn rat. Suddenly one of the kids sitting near the cage yelled out,

"Mrs. Hoagsbrith, the rat's gone! He's not in his cage!"

Instant pandemonium broke out in the room. There were shrieks and cries, and kids jumped onto their chairs and desks. Others scampered around the floor, looking for Squeak.

"There he is!" yelled someone, and the class erupted once again into yelling and screaming. Kids ran for the door while others chased the frightened rat. Mrs. Hoagsbrith froze, not sure whether to be one of the runners or the chasers. Books were knocked off the shelves and chairs were overturned. With kids stampeding in all directions, the barn rat dodged back and forth through the sea of legs trying desperately to find a way out of the room. There was a loud crash as someone accidently knocked over the goldfish bowl on the window ledge, sending Lucky the fish flying through the air and landing on the floor. Mrs. Hoagsbrith sprang forward in an effort to save Lucky. As the teacher raced across the room, the terrified rat lunged at her leg and ran up the back of her skirt, hoping to find a safe hiding spot. Mrs. Hoagsbrith screamed and shook her leg violently and then her entire body convulsed in some weird dance as she tried to shake the rat loose. As she pranced wildly about, her foot came down heavily on the poor goldfish and slid out from under her, knocking the teacher flat on her back and leaving a bright orange smear that had once been Lucky. Mrs. Hoagsbrith landed on the floor with a bone-jarring crunch.

Suddenly the whole class froze and fell silent, staring at the teacher on the floor. Breathlessly, we waited for Mrs. Hoagsbrith to move. Slowly she rolled into a sitting position and then stood up. A flat, furry pancake fell out from her skirt. Girls screamed and boys leaned over for a closer look.

"GO OUTSIDE FOR RECESS NOW!" shouted Mrs. Hoagsbrith between clenched teeth.

Everyone scrambled for the door. Once outside, we all

began to laugh and talk at once. Nothing like this had ever happened at Danglemore Public School before.

When we finally returned from our extended recess, the principal was in the classroom and he explained that Mrs. Hoagsbrith had gone home for the rest of the day.

That was the last time we ever studied animals in science class.

Chapter 6

Gordon's Rules

My friends and I love to play sports - soccer, football, hockey, basketball, baseball...You name it, we play it! We have two ways of playing sports: 1 - By the rules, and 2 - By Gordon's rules.

Take football, for example. It's usually Gordon, Paulo and me against Spot and Chopper. Now everyone knows dogs and turkeys can't catch or throw footballs, but they sure can tackle! Of course, Chopper can out-run all of us, and he tackles by grabbing the seat of our pants and dragging us down. The idea is to hand off the ball before this happens. Spot's trade-mark move is to hurl his fifty-pound body at you, and then scratch and peck at your body until you give up the ball (which you do pretty quickly). That's considered a down. A touchdown is scored if anyone manages to carry the ball for one full minute without losing it to either tooth or claw. For a field, we use the entire Lima farm. Nothing is out of bounds, and running through the cow pasture avoiding cows and cow paddies only adds to the skill and grit needed to play football by Gordon's rules.

The last time we played football, the game lasted for two hours without a single touchdown being scored. Our bodies ached from being turkey-tackled and the seats of our pants were torn from Chopper's teeth. We were exhausted and there was time for just one last play. Gordon drew us into a huddle.

"Guys," he said. "It's time to try our secret play, 'run-for-the-barn'."

With grim determination, Paulo and I nodded. We broke the huddle and lined up against Spot and Chopper.

I faced Spot, whose beady eyes glared at me. I glared menacingly back. Paulo was nose to muzzle with Chopper. Chopper's ears were laid back, his teeth were bared, and he growled at Paulo. Paulo bared his teeth and growled right back.

Drawing a deep breath, Gordon picked up the ball and started running backwards. Paulo tried to block Chopper, but the dog leapt sideways and darted around him. In an instant, he was on Gordon. I ran around Spot, and sprinted down the field towards the barn. Spot and Chopper pinned Gordon down, and the three of them wrestled on the ground, skin, fur and feathers flying. Suddenly, Gordon managed to roll over and toss the ball to Paulo, who quickly passed the football to me. I caught the ball and didn't look back. I raced towards the barn at full speed, with Spot in hot pursuit. Chopper ran around to the front of the barn to cut me off. As I raced around Big Boy's pen, Spot tackled me. We crashed to the ground and the ball flew out of my hands. It bounced and rolled out of sight around the corner, where Paulo's dad was sweeping the floor. The football rolled to a stop at his feet, and he casually bent over to pick it up. Just then, Chopper bounded into the barn. And then it happened. As Mr. Lima's hand came down over the ball, the football-crazy Chopper lunged at him and clamped his teeth into the seat of Mr. Lima's overalls. Mr. Lima yelped and reared up, just as Spot flung his body against the man, knocking him down. Trying desperately to shake himself free, Mr. Lima waved the football frantically in the air, which had the effect of waving a red flag in front of a bull. Spot and Chopper doubled the force of their attack. Just then, Paulo and Gordon ran into the barn.

"Pass! Pass!" cried Gordon.

Dazed, Mr. Lima tossed the ball to Gordon, who raced out of the barn with Spot and Chopper at his heels. Paulo and I took off towards the door, when suddenly Mr. Lima's hand reached out and stopped his son. I continued running out of the barn, leaving poor Paulo alone with his dad to explain how you play football by Gordon's rules.

Chapter 7

The Fart Chart

I don't remember exactly when Gordon invented the
Fart Chart, but I do remember when the Fart Chart got our
whole class in a lot of trouble. The Fart Chart was a list
that Gordon kept with every kid's name in the class on it.
Throughout the school day, whenever anyone passed
wind, Gordon would take out the list and put a checkmark
next to the kid's name. At the end of each week, kids
would stop Gordon and ask him how many points they
had accumulated. Naturally, it turned into a contest to see
who would be the first to reach 100. If our teacher, Mrs.

Hoagsbrith, noticed the increase in gas in the classroom, she didn't let on, and Gordon was very careful to keep the Fart Chart hidden.

It was the beginning of the second week of what had become known as the Great Farting Contest when things started getting out of hand. Over the weekend, someone discovered that eating large quantities of beans greatly increased the amount of times a person farted. This news spread through the class like wildfire, and I'm sure many parents were puzzled by their kids' sudden request for beans for breakfast, lunch and dinner. Some kids went as far as eating beans for snacks. By the middle of the week, we all sounded like giant bull frogs calling out to each other in the swamp. No sooner would one kid stop then another would start up. Mrs. Hoagsbrith pretended not to notice, but a fan appeared on her desk one day and she kept the windows wide open. She looked very relieved when the bell rang at the end of the day.

The next morning, all the kids gathered around Gordon while he read out the scores on the Fart Chart.

"It's going to be close," he announced. "Ten of you are

at an even 90, and most of the class is already over 80. If everyone gives it 100 per cent effort, we should have a winner by lunch time."

The bell rang and we all hurried into line, each of us eager to give it our best effort and be crowned the Farting Champion. We filed into our classroom and saw that we had a substitute teacher. (Apparently Mrs. Hoagsbrith was at home with a headache.) Being a substitute teacher is hard work at the best of times, but being a substitute teacher in our classroom during a farting contest is extremely challenging. This poor teacher never even made it until noon. By 9:15, the fan was on full-blast. By 9:30, the windows were wide open. At 10:00, she pulled a large bottle of aspirin out of her purse and swallowed several pills. She stared at the class in frustration as we all sat quietly in our seats, straining with the effort to become the Farting Champion.

The morning wore on, and still there was no champion. Some of the kids were even starting to look a little green themselves and the classroom reeked.

At recess, Gordon announced that four kids were tied

at 99 farts each. The next one to pass gas would be the Farting Champion. The bell rang and we entered our classroom. We were surprised to see the principal, Mr. Evans, standing at the front of the room.

"Your substitute teacher wasn't feeling well and she had to go home," he informed us. "So until another teacher can be found, I will be taking over." And then it happened.

A loud, long fart erupted from the back of the classroom. We all turned around to see who it was, and then the whole class erupted in cheering and shouting. Kids banged on their desks.

"YOU'RE THE NEW CHAMPION!" cried Gordon, forgetting to keep the Fart Chart hidden in his excitement. He raised his pencil to draw the last checkmark, when the paper was snatched out of his hands by Mr. Evans. Instantly the class was silent.

"What is the meaning of this?" demanded the principal, scanning the chart. Meekly, Gordon explained that it was a Fart Chart, and that everyone in the class was competing to be the new Farting Champion.

"No wonder your teachers keep going home sick!" said the principal. "Look at these figures! Gordon, you've never gotten 92 in anything at school in your life!"

Because everyone's name in the class was on the list, the whole class was in a whole lot of trouble. We were accused of making teachers sick on purpose, and all of our parents received a letter explaining what we had done. We were all given the task of writing a 500 word essay on the human body, explaining how the digestive system works. We also had to write letters to both Mrs. Hoagsbrith and the substitute teacher apologizing for making them sick. We didn't really mind though. The first annual Farting Champion had been crowned. Next year, we would just have to be sneakier!

Chapter 8

The Fair

Can throwing up ever be fun? Gordon, Paulo and I were about to find out. It was June, and the fair had come to town. We were standing in line for seats on the roller coaster, anxiously awaiting our turn. In our pockets, well-hidden from the man running the ride, were tightly-sealed sandwich bags of vegetable soup. Our plan, (naturally, it had been Gordon's idea) was simple and fool-proof. There was no way we could possibly get caught. I mean, how can you blame a kid for throwing up on a roller coaster?

The roller coaster finally came to a stop, and the passengers climbed out of their seats and made their way to the exit. Gordon, Paulo and I rushed through the turnstile and managed to get seats in the very first car. The three of us squeezed in and pulled the safety bar over our knees. We grinned at each other in anticipation. After everyone was seated and locked in, a big motor whirred and the cars slowly started to move. Rounding the first bend, we gathered speed, and the roller coaster chugged up a steep hill. The next instant, we were racing at breakneck speed down the hill, the wind whipping through our hair. People laughed and screamed as we flew along, fast as a rocket, taking sharp turns and twists. Suddenly, we were approaching the loop-the-loop.

"NOW!" Gordon yelled, and the three of us started making our best "kid-about-to-throw-up" sounds.

"Ooohhagh! Aaaagh! Blaaaaaaahh!"

"Ooowhaaah! Huuuu-aaaah!!"

Of course, we couldn't see behind us, but I expected that everyone on the ride was now wide-eyed with alarm.

51

Just imagine being trapped on a roller coaster racing toward the loop-the-loop knowing that someone ahead of you is about to throw up! We pulled our bags of soup out of our pockets in preparation.

The front of the roller coaster had just reached the top of the loop-the-loop when Gordon shouted the second command.

"Launch!!"

We zipped open our bags and shook out the contents into the air. The passengers immediately spotted the wet and chunky objects hurling toward them, and they frantically tried to duck, but there was nowhere to go. Soup rained down on them as we flew out of the loop-the-loop. There were cries of disgust and anguish, and then it happened. We heard the hacking sound of someone getting sick, and then another, and another. Getting thrown up on, (even if it was really only vegetable soup), was so disgusting that it was causing the passengers to throw up for real! It was our turn to get wide-eyed with alarm. We gasped as more and more people around us started throwing up. We had started the world's biggest chain-reaction hurl!

As the roller coaster tore around the track, vomit sprayed in all directions, soaking everyone in its path.

"I think I'm gonna be sick," groaned Gordon.

"DON'T YOU DARE!" I yelled at him. "This was your idea, anyway." Gordon didn't answer me, so I turned to look at him. He was green and his hair was wet and chunky. *Gross!* I touched my own hair. It, too, was wet and chunky. *Gross-er!*

Finally, the ride started to slow, and then it came to a stop. We joined the line of wet and chunky passengers as we moaned our way to the exit. The ride had to be closed while a clean-up crew hosed down the cars, and to this day, I still avoid roller coasters at the fair.

Chapter 9

The Camping Trip

It was June, and school was finally over. For months, Gordon, Paulo and I had been planning our first real camping trip. It had taken just as many months of begging our parents for permission to go on an overnight trip by ourselves, but finally they agreed that one night alone in the woods would be safe enough, and we were allowed to go. The only thing that Paulo's parents had insisted on was that we take Spot along with us.

"Spot?" I asked in surprise. "What good is a turkey going to do us on a camping trip?"

"Remember how he caught that burglar?" said Paulo. "Well, that's not all. My dad says that he's the best watch-turkey ever. He chases all the stray dogs off the farm. He barks, I mean, gobbles whenever anyone strange comes on the property, and he's wonderful at rounding up stray cattle. Just the other day --"

"All right, already," Gordon cut in. "He can come. But he sleeps in your sleeping bag!"

And that was that.

Early the next day, we packed all of our gear in Gordon's mom's mini-van. Fighting over who would get to sit in the front seat, we used our usual tactics - brute force and speed. We dashed to the mini-van tripping and tackling each other in our attempts to get to the vehicle first. Mrs. Smith appeared and ordered us to stop fighting.

"Spot will sit up front with me," she said. Grumbling, the three of us got into the back, while Spot, looking smug, hopped up front.

On the drive to the woods, we had a full half-hour lecture from Gordon's mom, starting with "Don't get lost:

Don't eat any strange berries: Don't keep food in your tent. It will attract racoons and bears." *Don't do this and don't do that.* Honestly, if parents spent as much time teaching their kids something useful as they did their *Don'ts,* we'd probably finish high school by the time we were twelve.

As the van rolled to a stop by the little one-lane bridge, we got the final "Don't."

"Whatever you do," warned Gordon's mother, "DON'T be late tomorrow! I'll be here to pick you up at 10:00am, and if you're not here, I'll assume you're lost and eating strange berries. Remember, 10:00 sharp!"

"Right. Bye, mom!" called Gordon.

"Bye, Mrs. Smith! Thanks for the ride," Paulo and I chorused, and with Spot leading the way, we entered the woods.

Right off the bat, I noticed Spot eating some strange berries as he led us down the trail. Come to think of it, Spot didn't know the way any better than we did, so why was he in the lead?

And another thing, I thought. *Spot's a turkey, and*

*turkey **is** food, so how come he's allowed to sleep with us in the tent?* We hadn't been gone five minutes, and already we had broken three *Don'ts*. This camping trip was going to be great!

Spot eventually led us to a nice, grassy spot in the middle of the forest next to a stream. We set up our tent, spread out our sleeping bags, hung our food in a tree and then raced off to explore the woods.

The day passed quickly. We returned to camp and fed Spot his grain and cooked hot dogs for ourselves over a small campfire. Once the fire was out, we decided to get our fishing rods and try our luck in the stream. Just as he was about to cast, Paulo slipped off of the mossy rock he was standing on, and landed in the water with a loud *SPLASH!* Gordon and I laughed so hard we had tears in our eyes, which made Paulo furious.

"Thanks for the help!" he said sarcastically as he waded ashore, soaked from head to foot. I reached out to give him a hand. Catching me off guard, Paulo pulled me into the stream with him, and it was his turn to laugh.

"There!" he cried triumphantly. "Now we're both

wet."

Sensing that he was next, Gordon dropped his fishing rod and ran into the bushes to hide.

Giggling, Paulo and I imitated Mrs. Smith's voice. "Gordon! Don't run away. It's time for your bath," I called in a high, squeaky voice.

"Come out, come out, wherever you are!" sang Paulo. Then I got an idea.

"Here, Spot!" I called, and the turkey waddled over. "Find Gordon. Where's Gordon?"

It only took a few minutes for Spot to sniff out Gordon.

"Good boy, Spot," said Paulo, as he and I pounced on Gordon and dragged him, kicking and screaming, to the stream and tossed him in. Now Spot was the only dry one among us, and he wisely flew out of reach onto a tree branch.

We stood on the bank of the stream, shivering, when Paulo suddenly looked at the sky and said, "Hey, guys, it's gonna be dark soon. We'd better hang up these wet clothes and get in the tent while we can still see."

We strung up a clothes line between two trees, stripped out of our wet things, and hung them on the line to dry overnight. We gathered up our fishing rods, and crawled into the tent. Figuring it was safe to come down out of his tree, Spot waddled into the tent and nestled at the foot of Paulo's sleeping bag. Exhausted from a long day, we were soon fast asleep. And then it happened. A sudden thunder clap exploded overhead, causing all of us to wake with a start. The wind, which had been a gentle breeze all day, suddenly had the force of a hurricane. The tent shook wildly, as though it might collapse, or worse, be carried away with the gale.

Gordon yelled, "Everyone take a corner and hold it down!" And everyone, including Spot, dove into a corner of the tent to keep it from becoming air-borne. The wind was too strong, however, and the tent whipped around like a leaf in the breeze. We clung to the corners for what seemed like hours before it finally began to die down.

"I think we can go back to sleep, now," said Paulo. "The worst seems to be over." We crawled gratefully back into our sleeping bags, and, more tired than ever, fell into a deep sleep.

The sun came up the next day, and the weather was clear and warm. Paulo, Gordon, Spot and I were so tired from the previous night's ordeal that we slept like babies and didn't wake up until nearly 9:00 o'clock. Jumping out of his sleeping bag, Gordon shouted, "Hurry up, guys. My mom'll kill us if we're late!" We dashed out of the tent. If we hurried, we could just make it to the bridge in time to meet Mrs. Smith. Suddenly, I froze and stared with horror at the clothes line. There was nothing on it! Not even a pair of socks!! The terrible wind had blown our clothes right off the line and carried them away! A quick search of the bushes revealed nothing, and we couldn't afford to waste any more time looking.

"What'll we do?" I asked.

"We'll have to walk back like this," said Gordon. "And we'd better hurry!"

Paulo and I started to protest, but Gordon interrupted. "Look, guys, we may be naked, but if we're not at that bridge by 10:00 sharp, we'll be naked *and dead!*"

Gordon was right. We packed up our tent and our

remaining gear, and hurried down the path to the bridge.

We arrived at the bridge at exactly five minutes to ten, and there was no sign of Gordon's mom. We crouched down behind the bushes at the side of the road to wait. A few minutes passed before we finally heard the crunch of tires on the gravel road. What we saw a moment later was worse than we had imagined. The thought of facing Gordon's mom naked was bad enough, but we hadn't bargained on Gordon's four sisters being in the van, too.

Five minutes later, the three of us were wrapped in a car blanket, sitting in the back of the van, while Gordon's sisters laughed uncontrollably. I think I even heard Mrs. Smith chuckle, too, although I couldn't be sure.

Chapter 10

The Burglar Trap

It was Gordon's idea, but then again, it usually was. The three of us were sitting in the tree fort in my back yard one afternoon. I had a real tree fort - the type that you could only get into by climbing a rope ladder that could be pulled up to keep out sisters, parents and kids we didn't like. We were talking about the latest excitement in the neighbourhood, a rash of burglaries. In the past two weeks, six houses had been broken into and computers were stolen. The police were on the lookout, but so far, they'd had no luck. As we talked, Gordon got more and more interested, and suddenly he exclaimed,

"Hey, guys. Let's catch the burglar ourselves. There's bound to be a reward!"

We were always looking for ways to earn some extra money, but this seemed like a matter for the police, not three kids.

"The police can't catch the crook, Gordon. How do you think we're going to?" demanded Paulo.

"That's easy," said Gordon confidently. "The police can't catch him because they have other things to do besides look for an old burglar. They're too busy looking for axe murderers and guys like that. But we've got nothing better to do all summer."

As it turned out, it didn't take all summer, only a week. I've got to hand it to Gordon. Sometimes his plans were pure genius, and this was one of his best.

"All we have to do," said Gordon, "is follow the clues we read in the newspapers and use those to catch him. He steals computers, right? Well, we'll use that clue to catch him."

"Brilliant," I said sarcastically. "But where are we

going to get a computer for him to steal. He's not taking mine."

"I'll explain on the way. Come on!" Gordon scampered down the rope ladder, quickly followed by Paulo and me.

We hopped on our bikes and pedalled to town. As we rode, Gordon explained.

"Catching a burglar is like catching a fish. You have to use the right bait, and we're going to the bait store."

I still didn't get it, but I rode along in ignorant silence until Gordon pulled his bike over beside the Mega Computer Store. Parking our bikes, we went inside and approached a big desk with a sign above it that read "Customer Service." Gordon politely asked the man behind the desk if there were any empty computer boxes that he might have.

"Sure," replied the man. "There's a whole garbage bin full of 'em behind the store. Help yourself."

"Thanks!" called Gordon over his shoulder as we departed the store and ran around back. Gordon sifted through the bin and came up with a large, heavy cardboard box. On the side was the name and model of a computer. All that was missing was the price tag, but anyone stealing computers would know that this was an expensive new one. Paulo grabbed a keyboard box and I grabbed one marked "19 -inch monitor". We were all set.

Riding back to my house with the big boxes proved to be difficult, but finally we reached my driveway. I still hadn't figured out how we were going to catch a burglar with empty boxes. We climbed back into the tree fort lugging the empty boxes and pulled up the ladder for extra security.

"What we do," explained Gordon when we were all seated on the floor, "is put these boxes in front of your house. The burglar will see them and think that you've bought an expensive new computer, which he'll then try to steal!"

"Hey, wait just a second!" I scowled. "Why *my* house? I don't want to get broken into. It's *always* my house!" I had memories of dead birds and bear tracks and the police showing up at my house. I didn't think my parents would appreciate me using our house as bait.

"Listen," Gordon continued. "It has to be your house because we just can't *see* the burglar steal the computer, we have to *catch him in the act*. And your house is the only one that will do."

Gordon continued to explain why my house was the perfect place to catch a thief. By the time he and Paulo went home for supper, I was convinced that Gordon's plan was a sure-fire one.

The next morning, we biked to the town dump and rummaged around until we found a dozen or so old bicycle tire inner tubes. These we hid in the tree fort along with the computer boxes. We pulled up the ladder and took inventory.

"Computer boxes?" asked Gordon

"Check," said Paulo

"Inner tubes?"

"Check."

"And I," said Gordon, "will supply the secret weapon!"

As I said, this was one of Gordon's best plans ever. Who but Gordon could capture a burglar with some empty boxes, a dozen inner tubes, and a huge pile of dirty diapers?

It took days for Gordon to collect enough diapers to put our plan into action, but at last we had a garbage bag full of smelly diapers (thanks to Gordon's baby sister) and we set to work.

First, the computer boxes were placed at the end of my driveway. The inner tubes were tied together into a long rubber rope, and then each end was tied to a tree.

With the three of us pulling as hard as we could, we stretched the inner tube rope into the fort, where we hooked it to a giant homemade pouch. Finally, we hooked the slingshot to a nail to hold it in place, ready to be loaded with dirty diapers.

Our trap was ready. We crouched in the tree fort and waited for action. Several hours went by and nothing happened. We decided to take breaks in shifts so we could stretch our legs. We ate some candy Paulo had brought along and talked about what we would do with the reward money. Still nothing happened. By five o'clock, neighbours started coming home from work, and we realized with sadness that my house would not be burglarized that day. We collected the computer boxes and hid them in the tree fort. Agreeing to meet first thing in the morning to try again, we called it a day.

Our burglar-watching continued for three more long days, and then it happened. On the fourth day of our burglar-watching, Gordon suddenly whispered,

"Hey, guys! Look!" He pointed to the back of my house. Sure enough, there was a strange man tip-toeing around the bushes, looking into windows. When he came to the back door, he glanced around to make sure he wasn't being watched, and then he pulled some small tools out of his pocket. He quickly picked the lock on the back door and slipped into the house.

"Quick! Get the sling-shot ready for action!" whispered Paulo excitedly.

With trembling fingers, we unhooked the giant pouch. It took the combined effort of Gordon and me to hold back the slingshot while Paulo dumped the bag of dirty diapers into the pouch to load it. The stench of dirty diapers filled the tree fort, causing us to gag. We aimed the slingshot at the back door and waited for the thief to come out of the house. I prayed he would ignore the old computer we kept in the basement and come out empty-handed. Either way, it didn't matter. We were going to catch him in the act! Five minutes later, the man opened the back door and glanced around the yard. He quietly stepped outside and shut the door behind him.

"Fire!" I shouted. We let go of the giant, smelly slingshot. Hearing my voice, the thief looked up just in time to see dozens of dirty diapers sailing through the air straight at him. He tried to duck, but the diapers were faster than he was. They flew at him and landed with wet, sticky, plopping sounds, knocking him completely off balance. The burglar fell hard, hitting his head and knocking himself unconscious. He lay motionless, sprawled on the deck, covered in wet, smelly diapers from head to foot.

We began to whoop and holler in the tree fort.

"We caught the burglar! We caught the burglar!" Gordon shouted.

Hearing the commotion, our neighbour, Mr. Butterworth, poked his head through the bushes and asked what the racket was all about.

"Call 9-1-1!" I shouted. "We caught the computer burglar!"

Mr. Butterworth charged into his house to call the police while we climbed out of the tree fort. In minutes, we could hear the distant sound of sirens growing louder as they approached my house. Suddenly the burglar regained consciousness and tried to stand up, floundering in the wet diapers. Hearing the sirens, he attempted to run for it. He slipped and skidded across the deck, and tore off down the driveway. Gordon, Paulo and I took off after him.

"Don't let him get away!" I shouted.

At that moment, four police cruisers came to a sudden stop in front of my house. The burglar saw that he was trapped and gave up. Slowly he raised his dirty hands in the air, and the police, gagging on the stench, placed him in handcuffs.

Gordon, Paulo and I were heroes. We each got a certificate and $200.00 dollars! We spent the rest of the summer dreaming of ways to spend our reward money.

Chapter 11

The Big Fish

Every summer our town holds a fishing derby with a thousand dollar grand prize for the biggest catch. This year, Gordon, Paulo and I were determined to win. Gordon borrowed his Uncle Ivan's huge fishing rod that he used for ocean fishing, explaining that if you wanted to catch big fish, you had to use big gear and big bait.

As Gordon's dad drove us out to the lake, he gave us a pep talk and some fishing tips, and finished with a lecture on good sportsmanship.

" ...and don't be too disappointed if you don't win," he said. "I think your equipment is too big for any fish in this lake."

Ignoring his last comment, we cheerfully said good-bye and carried our gear down to the water. Gordon unwrapped a large hunk of meat and stuck it on a big shark hook at the end of the rod. It took all of his strength to cast the huge bait into the deep water of the lake.

We sat on the shore, each taking turns holding the heavy rod. Hours passed without a single strike. The lake was busy with sailboats and canoes. People in motorboats tried their luck at catching "the big one" and then headed off towards other parts of the lake. Growing bored, I looked at my watch. It was 11:30. Gordon's dad would be back to pick us up at noon.

"We've been skunked," I started to say, and then it happened. The little bell on the tip of the rod began to ring, signaling a fish on the line. Gordon jumped to his feet, the rod grasped firmly in both hands. Line began to slowly unwind from the spool as the fish carried away the bait. When the line suddenly stopped, Gordon lowered the rod tip to the water and quickly reeled in the slack. With all his might, he jerked the rod up, setting the hook, while Paulo and I shouted instructions. The fish responded violently, pulling Gordon toward the lake. Paulo and I jumped to his aid and with the three of us holding the rod, we were able to keep Gordon from being pulled into the water.

"It's huge!" exclaimed Gordon.

"Bet it's the winner!" I shouted. "Don't let him get away!"

The giant fish pulled harder and we were dragged forward again.

"HOLD ON!" screamed Paulo.

We dug in and managed to regain our ground, the fish putting up the fight of its life. The battle see-sawed like this for several more minutes and we began to tire. The fish tugged violently and we were dragged in up to our ankles. Another sharp tug from the fish and we were wet up to our knees. One more pull and we'd be waist-deep. Suddenly we heard Gordon's dad shouting to us.

"Hold on, boys! I'm coming to help." He splashed

into the water and grasped the rod. Slowly, he began to heave us back to shore. The huge fish was no match for the four of us. Steadily, we began to reel him in. With one last giant effort, the fish was pulled to the surface of the water. We stared in stunned silence and our jaws dropped in amazement. Our huge fish began to stand up. Our "big catch" was not a fish at all. What we had caught was a scuba diver! The sharp hook was firmly snagged on the seat of his wet-suit.

For a long moment, no one said a word. Disappointment settled over Gordon, Paulo and me like a dark cloud. Behind us, Gordon's dad started to chuckle. The scuba diver removed his helmet and he too began to laugh.

"Well, guys," he said. "You caught the big one, alright. It's a shame you can't enter *me* in the contest. You'd win for sure 'cause I weigh 180 pounds!"

That gave Gordon an idea, and his face suddenly lit up.

"Wait a minute! The rules said 'prizes for the biggest catch.' It didn't say exactly *what* you had to catch!"

By now, people had gathered around us, and they

began nodding their heads in agreement. It didn't take much arguing to convince the judges either, and Gordon, Paulo and I were awarded the grand prize - $1000.00, which we split with the scuba diver so he could buy a new wet-suit.

Chapter 12

Practical Jokes

Gordon's dad is the king of practical jokes, and Gordon has learned a lot from his father. Surviving April Fool's Day at Gordon's house is like dodging land mines - salt in the sugar bowl, itching powder in your underwear, and powdered drink mix in the shower head so that when you turn on the water, you get a purple shower!

One day when we were hanging out at my house with nothing to do, Gordon suggested we make some crank phone calls.

"It's fun! I do it all the time," said Gordon. "Watch."

He picked up the phone and dialed a number at random. After two rings, a lady answered.

"Hello. Is Jim home?" asked Gordon.

"I'm sorry. There's no Jim here," said the lady.

"Oh, sorry to have bothered you," said Gordon politely and he hung up.

"What's so funny about that?" demanded Paulo.

"Wait," replied Gordon. He picked up the phone and hit the redial button.

"Hello?" came the lady's voice again.

"May I speak to Jim, please?" said Gordon.

"You've got the wrong number again," came the voice, a little less patiently this time.

"I'm so sorry. I'll double-check the number," said Gordon and he hung up.

"Oh, that's hilarious," I said sarcastically.

"Just wait," said Gordon coolly, and a few minutes later, he dialed the lady's number again.

"Can I speak to Jim?" he asked.

"Look," said the lady. "For the third time, there's no Jim at this number!" *CLICK!*

Gordon hung up the phone, laughing. "Boy, she's really mad," he said.

"Yeah, but what so funny about that?" I asked.

"You'll see," was Gordon's reply. Ten minutes later he dialed the number again. When the lady answered, he said, "Hello. This is Jim. Have there been any calls for me?" He slammed down the receiver and burst out laughing. Paulo and I laughed, too.

"That was pretty good!" said Paulo.

"Yeah, I want to try it!" I said, grabbing the phone.

"I don't know if you're ready," said Gordon.

"What do you mean, *ready*?" I demanded.

"It's not as easy as it looks," said Gordon.

"Sure it is!" I said. I just watched you do it, didn't I?"

"Well," said Gordon hesitantly. "At least let me dial for you. He quickly punched in a number. The phone rang several times before a man answered.

"Hello. Is Jim home?" I asked.

"Speaking," said the man. I froze and looked at Gordon. *Now what?* I slammed down the receiver. Gordon was doubled over with laughter.

"Boy, did you fall for it!" he gasped between bursts of laughter. Slowly it dawned on me that Gordon had set me up.

"You mean you *knew* that someone named Jim lived at the number?!" I shouted.

"Yeah!" said Gordon. "Great joke, eh?" He burst out laughing again and Paulo joined in, too.

"That's not funny!" I said. "I'll get you back for this!"

"O-o-o-h, I'm so scared," said Gordon smirking. "I'd like to see you try!"

That's how the war of the practical jokes began.

*   *   *

A few days later, Paulo and I went fishing. Gordon was supposed to go with us, but he called to say he wasn't feeling well and wouldn't be joining us. I didn't entirely believe this story, but Paulo said to quit worrying about Gordon and his practical jokes.

We fished hard all morning but by noon we still hadn't caught a thing.

"I've got to head home anyway and do the chores," said Paulo. "My parents are away all day and I've got a lot of extra work to do."

"I'll give you a hand," I offered. (Doing other kids' chores is always more fun that doing your own, and I had nothing better to do, anyway).

"Great!" said Paulo and we hopped on our bikes and pedaled to his house.

"First I have to feed the pig," said Paulo when we arrived at the farm. "The chickens don't get fed until later." We entered the barn. Paulo picked up a bucket and we headed to Big Boy's pen. Suddenly, we both stopped and froze in our tracks. The gate to the pen was ajar, and there was no sign of the pig! We both began calling out Big Boy's name and frantically searching the barn.

"I know I closed that gate this morning!" insisted Paulo. "There's no way he could have opened it himself." We ran outside and searched the entire farm, but there was no sign of the pig. "My parents will kill me when they get home," exclaimed Paulo.

"Well, how far could he have gone?" I asked. "Let's go ask the farmer next door if he saw Big Boy."

"Your pig got loose?" said the farmer when we asked if he'd seen Big Boy. "I've never heard of a pig getting loose. Cows and horses, yes, but never a pig." We went home dejected.

"I'm dead," said Paulo sadly.

"It wasn't your fault," I said, trying to cheer him up. "Maybe somebody stole him!"

"Yeah," said Paulo brightening. "I bet you're right!" Now that Paulo figured he might not be blamed for leaving the pen open, he felt a little better. We decided to play computer games until it was time to feed the chickens.

The minute we entered Paulo's house, a horrible smell hit us, a smell not unlike a pig pen.

"Where's that stench coming from?" demanded Paulo, running from room to room. All of a sudden he let out a yell. I ran over to where he stood and followed his gaze into his own bedroom. To my shock, there was Big Boy lying on Paulo's bed, his head nestled on the pillow! All of a sudden, from out of the closet, jumped Gordon.

"**Gotchya!!**" he yelled, and he fell over laughing.

Paulo was furious.

"I told you you'd never get me!" sang Gordon.

It took Paulo and I ten minutes to get the pig off the bed and back into his pen.

"We've got to get Gordon back," grumbled Paulo.

"I know, but how?" I asked.

"I'm not sure yet, but you just wait!"

I've never seen Paulo so determined in my life.

*   *   *

Several days passed before Paulo came up with a plan, but when he finally did, it was perfect. It was so good, I would have sworn it was Gordon's own idea. It didn't take us long to gather up the necessary tools to pull off the prank. Early in the morning we collected all the fresh cow patties we could find on Paulo's farm and fill a paper bag with them. We grabbed a lighter and headed off toward Gordon's house.

Our timing was perfect. Mr. Smith always left early for work at the hospital, and Mrs. Smith was just leaving as Paulo and I approached the house, crouching down in the bushes across the road as she passed by in her car.

Gordon's sisters were away at camp, so that just left Gordon at home. We crept up to the front porch, carefully set the bag down and lit a corner of it with the lighter. When the flame caught and the whole bag began to burn, we rang the doorbell and took off across the street, hiding in the bushes again to watch the action. We waited for Gordon to open the door, see the fire and stomp it out with his feet, covering himself with fresh cow manure. And then it happened. The front door swung open, and there stood not Gordon, but his father, who hadn't gone to work early after all! He saw the flames, gave a surprised yell and began stomping on the fiery bag. With each stomp, manure sprayed out of the bag, covering the front porch, the bricks, and Mr. Smith! The fire was quickly put out, and Mr. Smith stood on his porch staring at the mess and cursing. Paulo and I sat silently in the bushes not knowing quite what to do, when all of a sudden, a voice behind us made us both jump.

"I told you you'd never get me!"

We whirled around to see Gordon standing behind us, grinning triumphantly.

About the Authors

Michael Wade was born a long time ago, in a place far, far away. He grew up in London, Ontario and currently lives in Strathroy, Ontario. Michael enjoys hunting, wilderness canoeing and working out.

Laura Wade was born not quite so long ago and not as far away as Michael. She, too, was raised in London, Ontario and currently resides in Strathroy, where she works as a Children's Librarian.